BEAUTY AND THE BEAST

RETOLD AND ILLUSTRATED BY WARWICK HUTTON

A MARGARET K. MCELDERRY BOOK

ATHENEUM   1985   NEW YORK

This Book is for Lily

Library of Congress Cataloging in Publication Data

Hutton, Warwick.
Beauty and the beast.
"A Margaret K. McElderry book."
Summary: Through her great capacity to love, a kind
and beautiful maid releases a handsome prince from the
spell which has made him an ugly beast.
[1. Fairy tales.   2. Folklore—France]   I. Title.
PZ8.H98Be   1985   398.2'0944 [E]   84-48441
ISBN 0-689-50316-4

Published simultaneously in Canada by McClelland & Stewart, Ltd.
Manufactured by Dai Nippon Printing Company in Japan
Composition by Dix Type Inc., Syracuse, New York

First Edition

Deep in the country, there once lived a merchant who had fallen on hard times. He had three daughters. The older two were ill-tempered and dissatisfied with their father's bad luck, but the youngest—called Beauty for her lovely face—made the best of the situation and tried hard to keep the rest of the family happy.

One day, the merchant heard that a ship was due to come into port. He hoped it would have rich cargo on board that he had ordered while he was still wealthy. Praying his fortunes would take a turn for the better, he made ready to go off to the seaport. Before he left, his two older daughters begged him to buy clothes and finery for them with the money he expected to make. But Beauty, whose needs were always more modest, could think of asking only for a rose.

Once again the merchant was unlucky with his affairs, and he set off on the homeward journey in low spirits. Bad weather followed him. The sky darkened and he lost his way. Distraught at losing both his luck and now his way, he rode on through dense and gloomy shadows, until a terrible storm broke around him.

The rain and sleet lashed down, and he was beginning to think he might die in the storm when, deep in a forest, he came to a long avenue of trees with a small light glimmering at the end.

He hurried toward it and found a house so magnificent it seemed like a palace. After stabling his horse, he entered a large room with a blazing fire and a meal set out, ready for one person. Yet however loudly and however often he called, no one appeared. At length, hungry and exhausted, he sat down to eat the food. Then, feeling braver, he explored further, until he found a bedroom in which to rest.

In the morning, he was astonished to discover a new cloak laid out with his own clothes, which had been carefully dried. Where there had been supper the evening before, breakfast had now appeared, and in wonderment he ate, quite convinced that the house belonged to some kind of magician.

On the way to the stable to get his horse, he passed a rosebush and, thinking of Beauty, he picked some. No sooner were the roses in his hands than the peace and tranquillity of the sunlit morning were shattered by a most terrible roar. A monstrous beast came out from behind the rosebush, crying in a terrible voice, "I have fed you, clothed you, and cared for you, but now I see you are a thief. You must die!"

"Oh my lord, I promised to take back a rose for one of my daughters. That is the only reason I have picked these," said the poor merchant.

"Don't call me lord. I am a beast and know it, but if you have daughters, let one of them come to live here willingly, in your place, and I will forgive you. Promise now or die at once."

The terrified man agreed to bring back one of them in exchange for his life or to return himself to die.

When he reached home he could scarcely bear to tell his daughters of his dreadful promise, but Beauty saw how troubled he was, and begged him to tell them his extraordinary story. At once Beauty insisted on going to the beast's palace in her father's place. He had, after all, picked the roses for her. And though her father had in truth planned to return himself, nothing would change Beauty's decision. Her sisters were secretly relieved, but her father was heartbroken. Still hoping in some way to escape the beast's anger, he set off with her the next day.

When they arrived at the palace that evening, it was as empty and silent as before, only this time a meal for two was laid ready. While they were eating, a terrible roar was heard once more and the Beast appeared.

"Do you come here willingly?" he asked Beauty.

"Yes, I do," she replied, faint with terror.

"I am glad of that. Your father may stay tonight, but when he goes tomorrow, he must never return here again." Then with a great groan the Beast withdrew.

Beauty and her father found bedrooms for the night and in fear and sadness settled down to sleep. To Beauty's surprise, she slept well. In her dreams, a fine lady appeared who told her not to despair, promising she would be rewarded for her unselfishness. The lady seemed so kind and reassuring that, in the morning, at her father's tearful departure, Beauty told him she knew she would be safe and well, and he seemed to gain some comfort from her words.

Now alone, Beauty wandered through the huge palace. In one wide corridor, she noticed a large door with "Beauty's Rooms" inscribed above. Surprised, she entered and found living rooms, bedrooms, and a large library. Everything seemed prepared for her, but though it was beautiful and inviting, she could not help sighing. "Oh, if only I could see my father," she said. As she uttered these words, her gaze fell on a great mirror in which, through a mist, she saw the merchant arriving home safely.

The days passed uneventfully into weeks. The palace seemed always perfectly kept, although no servants ever appeared, and Beauty lived happily in the peace and quiet of the many magnificent rooms and lovely gardens.

Each morning, new dresses were put out ready for Beauty to wear, and, each evening, the Beast would come and ask if she had everything she wanted.

"Do you think I am very ugly?" he would mournfully ask, and she would answer, "None could call you handsome." Groaning sadly, he would vanish. Sometimes he would ask further if she liked him, and as Beauty had begun to feel how gentle and thoughtful he was, she would reply, "Yes, your heart is good. I no longer fear your looks." But when he asked if she would ever consider marrying him, the thought so shocked her that she could not reply. Then the Beast groaned most mournfully.

Her life was full of lovely things, but Beauty was lonely, and soon she came to look forward to her evening meetings with the Beast.

One morning, when she looked again into the magic mirror, she was shocked to see an image of her father lying ill. At supper it was plain to the Beast that Beauty was pining for her home. "If you leave me," the Beast said, "I will slowly die. However, I cannot bear to see you so unhappy. Go back to your father."

"No," replied Beauty. "You have been so kind and faithful that I cannot cause your death. I promise to go for only one week."

The Beast gave her a ring that would instantly return her to his palace when she took it off her finger and told her that she would be at her father's house in the morning.

At dawn, as the Beast had promised, Beauty awoke in her old home. Her father wept for joy at seeing her again. While Beauty was away, her two sisters had married, but they were as dissatisfied as ever. When they saw how peaceful and happy she was, they soon determined in their jealousy to stop Beauty from returning to the Beast's palace.

Although Beauty had promised to stay at home only for a week, her sisters pretended to need her greatly to care for their father who now lived alone. Ten days passed before she began to worry about the Beast. That night she dreamed that he had fallen to the ground in the garden she knew so well and lay groaning in despair. When she awoke she remembered his words—that he would die if she did not return. Quickly she pulled off the ring he had given her and fell asleep once more.

In the morning she awoke in her rooms at the Beast's palace. All was as calm and beautiful as before, and the day passed quietly as so many others had. The Beast always appeared at suppertime, so Beauty waited for the evening impatiently. At long last the wished-for time came, yet still she was alone. With growing fear she began to search the rooms of the palace. Then, remembering her dream, she ran to the gardens. There she searched the many terraces, paths, and lawns until at last she found the Beast stretched out on the ground. He was scarcely breathing.

Beauty knelt beside him, in terror for his life, crying, "I should never have left you!"

The Beast's eyes opened briefly and he said, "I shall die happily now that I have seen you again."

Beauty cried, "Oh Beast, please live, I cannot bear to lose you! I want to marry you and live here for ever . . ."

As she said these words, the palace seemed to sparkle with light, and while Beauty watched, the Beast, who had been dying, slowly changed. There beside her lay a young and handsome prince. Slowly he sat up. Then he told her how he had been turned into a beast by a wicked fairy and condemned to remain so until a young maiden promised to marry him.

Arm in arm, they went into the palace where Beauty's father and sisters had been summoned. The Beast told them how Beauty's love of character instead of looks had broken the evil spell, and in a few days the wedding of Beauty and her prince took place. It is true to say that, except for the two jealous older sisters, all lived happily for many long years.